II

A NEST OF BLUEBIRDS

Rose Marie Botts Scott

The Wooster Book Company
Wooster Ohio • 2001

The Wooster Book Company

where minds and imaginations meet

205 West Liberty Street
Wooster Ohio • 44691
www.woosterbook.com

ISBN 1-888683-41-4

Carlisle Printing

WALNUT CREEK

This book tells the true story of the bluebirds that nested in a birdhouse in my backyard. I grew up on a farm in Indiana during the 1930s and it was there I learned to love and appreciate nature.

My mother had a bluebird house on the fence around her garden and every summer the bluebirds returned to that house to nest and sing for us. My mother taught me to enjoy watching the bluebirds and listening to their song. My mother had a love for the birds, as well as all of the wonders of nature and all of God's creations that she passed on to her children.

Now I am 76 years old and I have a bluebird house in my garden. I watch the bluebirds and keep a diary of their activities. I am so impressed by their natural intelligence and cleverness that I decided to tell their story. I hope you will enjoy learning about bluebirds as much as I have enjoyed drawing and telling their story.

ROSE

A Note to Parents and Teachers:

The text of this book is designed so that it can be understood by both young children and older readers. The simple story told on the right-hand pages is easily understood by a young child. Text on the left-hand pages is intended to be used as an educational tool to enhance the story.

This book
is dedicated to
my loving
Mother's
Memory

VIII

A Nest of Bluebirds

Bluebirds usually arrive in the northern states in early spring when there is food for them to eat. They eat insects like grasshoppers, crickets, ground beetles, and cater-pillars. They also like summer berries, chopped raisins, and meal worms.

One spring morning, there they were! A pair of
beautiful bluebirds in my yard.

*If you want to attract bluebirds,
put the house in an open area,
four or five feet off the ground.
Fence rows on the edges of fields
or pastures are ideal places.*

Soon they were going in and out of the birdhouse. I could see them from my kitchen window.

The male bluebird is more colorful than the female bluebird, with brighter blue and orange feathers.

How do you like this neighborhood? Shall
we move in?

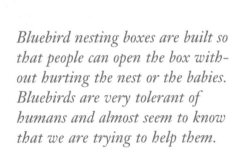

Bluebird nesting boxes are built so that people can open the box without hurting the nest or the babies. Bluebirds are very tolerant of humans and almost seem to know that we are trying to help them.

It took a week for the bluebirds to decide if they really wanted to move in. Every morning they would visit, going in and out of the house, just like they were trying to decide. Then a pair of sparrows decided they wanted the house too. Every time the sparrows would go in the bird-house, I would go outside and chase them away. The bluebirds seemed to know I was helping them.

ROSE

*Wrens and sparrows
will often try to take
over a bluebird box.
Try to keep the box far
from woods and barn-
yards—the places
wrens and sparrows
like to live.*

One day the sparrows were being very defiant.
What I saw next was amazing! The male bluebird
flew away and returned with five or six other male
bluebirds. They all started diving at the sparrows
until the sparrows gave up and left.

Bluebirds are cavity nesters—they build their nests in a box or a hollow tree. Since bluebirds cannot make the cavity, like a woodpecker, they have to find one ready-made.

Mother bluebird
begins to build the
nest. She starts
with small twigs
and then grasses.
She lines the nest
with soft materials
like feathers.

The female bluebird builds the
nest by herself. The male bluebird
may bring her a few sticks to help.
It takes from two to five days to
build the nest.

Father bluebird sits near the nest and sings,
watching over the birdhouse and mother bluebird,
to protect them. The bluebird's song is a simple
song of a few notes.

In mid-April, the female bluebird will lay one egg early in the morning each day. She spends the rest of the day away from the nest looking for food. When all the eggs are laid, she will begin sitting on the eggs, so that all the eggs will hatch at the same time.

The mother bluebird lays one egg each day until there are four to six eggs in the nest.

The female sits on the eggs all night and may leave the nest during the day for short periods. If the weather is warm, she may spend more time away from the nest. The female will gently turn the eggs to keep them evenly warm during the incubation time..

While mother bluebird sits on the eggs, father bluebird guards the nest and brings insects for her to eat. "Yum, yum! A tasty caterpillar!"

The eggs will hatch in 12–14 days. Baby bluebirds break through the shell with their "egg-tooth"—a hard part of their upper bill.

On a warm day, when mother and father bluebird are away from the nest, I opened the box to see that there were five sky-blue eggs.

When the eggs hatch, the baby bluebirds have no feathers. The mother sits on the babies to keep them warm until they grow soft feathers, called down. This takes about five days.

When the eggs hatch, the babies' eyes are closed. They have wobbly heads but very big mouths! I open the bird-house door very carefully to take a peak at the baby birds. I am careful not to spend too much time looking or open the door too often. The babies are very fragile.

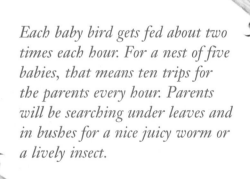

Each baby bird gets fed about two times each hour. For a nest of five babies, that means ten trips for the parents every hour. Parents will be searching under leaves and in bushes for a nice juicy worm or a lively insect.

Mother and father bluebird are very busy finding insects to feed their babies. The baby birds have to grow quickly. Before the summer is over, they must be able to fly many miles to a warmer climate.

At first, the babies are fed soft insects, like caterpillars and spiders. Later they will get grasshoppers, crickets, beetles, and berries.

"Feed me! Feed me!"

*Bluebirds keep the nest clean.
When the eggs hatch, they take
the eggshells out of the nest. Fecal
sacs from the babies—the "dirty
diapers"—are flown away from
the nest by the parents.*

$\mathcal{T}$he parents also clean out the nest. Here is father bluebird taking out the "dirty diapers."

Now the baby blue-birds move around in the nest box a lot, stretching their wings. They do not have to learn how to fly, they already know how.

Two weeks old and the babies have almost outgrown the nest! Those insects and worms must be very nutritious.

After the eggs hatched, I could raise the door of the birdhouse every few days to get a closer look at the babies. Since the parents seemed to know me as their friend, they didn't seem to mind.

"Feed me first, Mom!"

While the babies are in the nest, I open the nesting box once a week and check under the nest material for blowfly larvae. The larvae can attach themselves to the baby bluebirds as a parasite and injure the babies.

*T*he young bluebirds poke their heads out of the nesting box door to watch for their parents. "It's getting crowded in here."

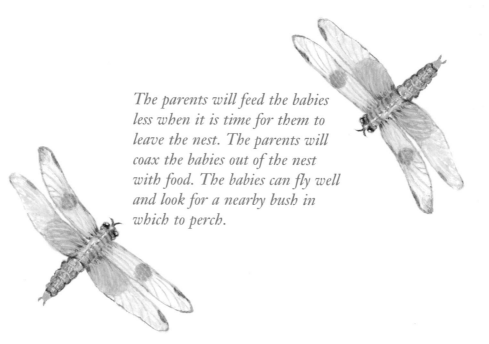

*The parents will feed the babies
less when it is time for them to
leave the nest. The parents will
coax the babies out of the nest
with food. The babies can fly well
and look for a nearby bush in
which to perch.*

*N*ow, the baby birds are as big as their parents and are ready to leave the nest. Early in the morning, one little bird looks out of the nesting box. The parents are sitting nearby. The first little bird bravely takes it's first solo flight. Soon another bird follows. They won't return to the birdhouse and will now live in the trees.

The little birds are fluffy balls of feathers with spotted breasts. Only a few feathers are blue on the tips of the wings and tails. At this age, the birds are called fledglings.

Soon all five babies are out of the box.
They all call to their parents to feed them.

Now that the young birds have left the nest, the parents take the babies into the bushes where it is safer. The babies call from their hiding places so their parents can find them and feed them. Later, the young bluebirds will fly into the fields and the parents will show the babies how to find food.

"What's for dinner, Mom? Is that
a caterpillar or a grasshopper? Will
you teach me how to catch one?"

When all the babies had left the nest, I cleaned out the box to get it ready for another family of bluebirds. In a couple of weeks, the parent bluebirds came back to the house and the young birds came along to watch.

Mother and father bluebird are ready to start another family this summer. The children come along to watch their parents search for a place to build a new nest.

The young bluebirds watch their mother picking up nesting material. They pick at the twigs and grass, copying her, but they do not help build the new nest.

$\mathcal{J}$ust like before, the parents look over the nesting box, going in and out. Mother bluebird shows her children what to use to make the nest, picking just the right soft twig or feather.

The first batch of young bluebirds often helps feed the babies in the second nest. They also help protect the nest from enemies. When the new babies leave the nest, they fly with their parents and sisters and brothers to find food.

*A*gain, mother bird lays five blue eggs in the nest. Father bird feeds her and guards the nest. When the eggs hatch, the young birds help feed the new babies.

When the weather starts to get cold, bluebirds usually migrate south. They will sometimes stay through the winter if there are berries to eat. Several bluebirds will huddle together in nesting boxes to keep warm through the winter.

ROSE

 $\mathcal{N}$ ow it is fall and all the bluebirds return to my yard. They visit the back-yard each morning for a week or more, looking over my birdhouse for next year. Maybe they are saying, "Thank you!" and "We'll see you next Spring!"

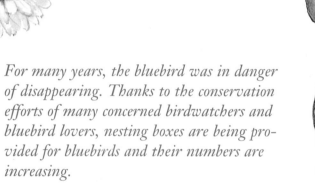

For many years, the bluebird was in danger of disappearing. Thanks to the conservation efforts of many concerned birdwatchers and bluebird lovers, nesting boxes are being provided for bluebirds and their numbers are increasing.

At one time, bluebirds were almost extinct due to the use of pesticides and the loss of nesting places.

The End

Rose Marie Scott lives in Fort Wayne Indiana and did not plan to write and illustrate this story. After watching these little bluebirds all summer and remembering what she had seen during the winter months, she started painting some of the things she had watched the bluebirds doing. Next, she added captions to the pictures to explain each picture. One thing led to another. "I got so involved in the project, it became a passion."

After raising a family of three daughters and retiring from the workplace, Rose Marie had time to pick up the paintbrush and devote time to one of her favorite pastimes.

"I am an old fashioned housewife who enjoys keeping house, baking bread from scratch, keeping busy with knitting, tending to my flower garden, finding time for artwork, and playing the piano—as well as enjoying time spent playing golf with my husband Don."